Cc Dd

f Gg

Kk Ll Mm

For my wingman, Neal

Copyright © 2017 by Stephen Savage
A Neal Porter Book
Published by Roaring Brook Press
Roaring Brook Press is a division of Holtzbrinck Publishing Holdings Limited Partnership
175 Fifth Avenue, New York, New York 10010
The artwork for this book was created using digital techniques.
mackids.com

Library of Congress Contol Number: 2016035668

ISBN: 978-1-62672-436-5

Our books may be purchased in bulk for promotional, educational, or business use. Please
contact your local bookseller or the Macmillan Corporate and Premium Sales Department
at (800) 221-7945 ext. 5442 or by e-mail at MacmillanSpecialMarkets@macmillan.com.

First edition 2017
Printed in China by Toppan Leefung Printing Ltd., Dongguan City, Guangdong Province

1 3 5 7 9 10 8 6 4 2

Little Plane

LEARNS to WRITE

STEPHEN SAVAGE

A NEAL PORTER BOOK
ROARING BROOK PRESS
NEW YORK

and his arcs,

but
loopity-loops
made him
dizzy.

The next morning
Little Plane tried his best.

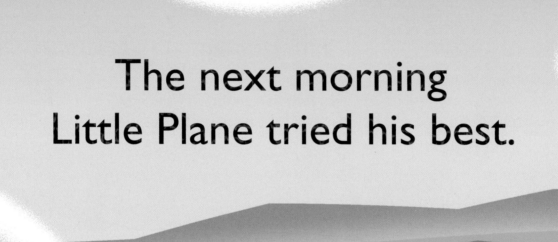

"Where's your loopity-loop?"
asked the flight instructor.

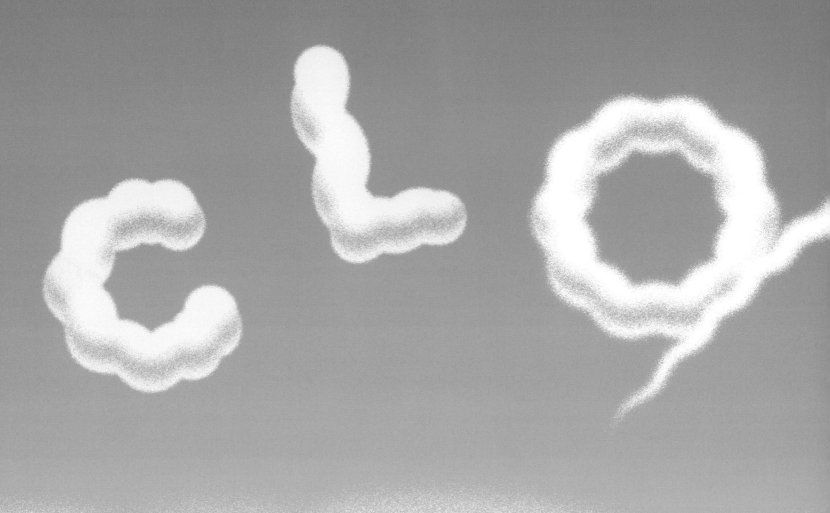

And Little Plane did.

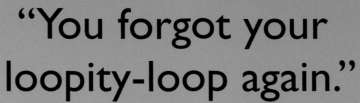

"You forgot your
loopity-loop again."

"Writing is too hard,"
thought Little Plane.
Then, the moon appeared.

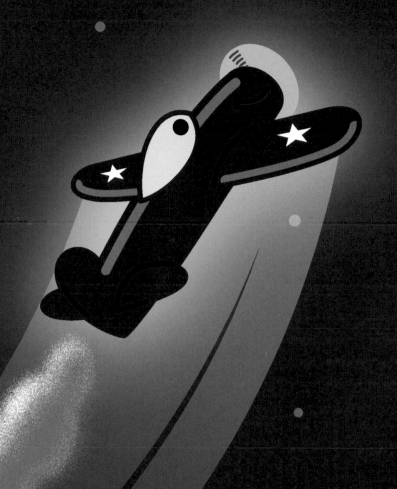

He flew around it
very carefully . . .

And made
a perfect
loopity-loop.
Then he made
another one,
and he didn't
even get dizzy.

Little Plane
had learned
to write!

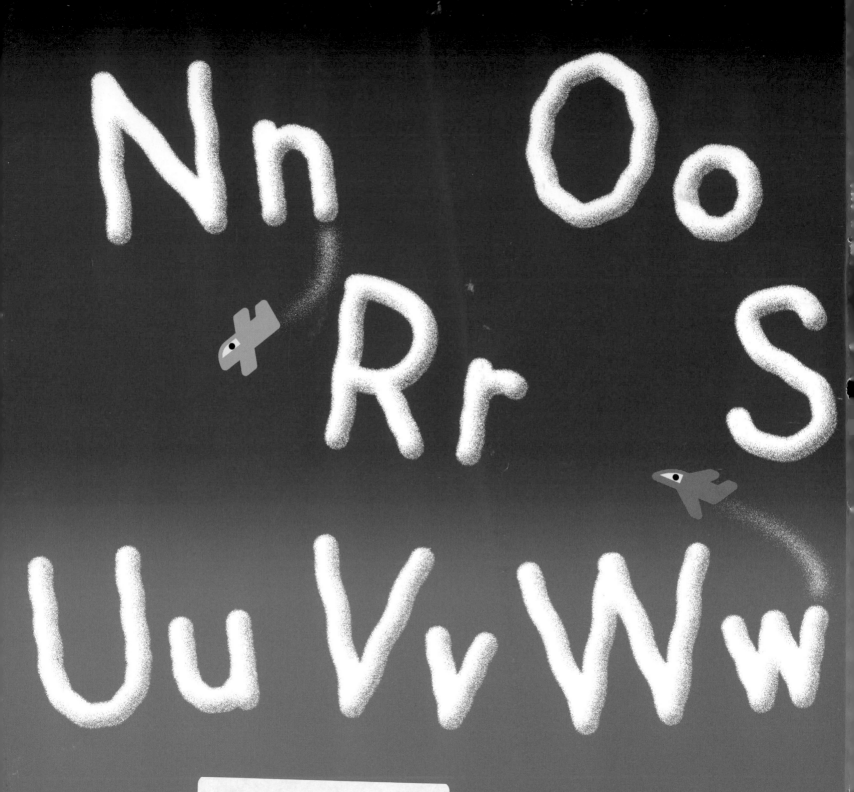